Paul Revere's Ride

by

Henry Wadsworth Longfellow

Illustrated by Monica Vachula

Historical Note by Jayne E. Triber, Ph.D.

Boyds Mills Press

In memory of my brother
— M. V.

In appreciation:

Sergeant Paul Tobin and Trooper Andrew Tobin of the
Massachusetts National Lancers deserve special thanks for
their cheerful and willing cooperation, as each in turn brought
to life the ride of Paul Revere. Special thanks also to Paul
Comptois, Susan Rockwell, Susan Morse, and Audrey Hasford of
the Lexington Historical Society for being so generous with their
time and expertise, and for allowing me access to their sites
and activities. At the Longfellow Historical Site, National Park
Service, in Cambridge, Massachusetts, T. Michele Clark and
Paul Blandford graciously went out of their way to accommo-
date my requests. Marcia Moss, who for thirty-six years served
as Town Archivist and the Curator of Special Collections at the
Concord Free Public Library, shared with me her extensive
knowledge of local history and pointed me in the right direc-
tion more than once. I would also like to thank Dr. and Mrs.
Joseph E. D. Humphries, and Mr. and Mrs. Loring Coleman for
providing me with authentic costumes, period props, and very
entertaining tales. Darcy McCurdy and Bean gave liberally and
with good humor of their time and their boating expertise. I
am deeply and forever grateful to Larry Rosler of Boyds Mills
Press for his patience and understanding, to Dr. Jon DuBois
and Dr. Lynn Weigel for keeping me going, and to my family
and friends for their many kindnesses in word and in deed.
Most of all, I would like to thank my husband, George, for
everything.

— M. V.

Illustrations © 2003 by Monica Vachula
Historical note © 2003 by Jayne Triber, Ph.D.
All rights reserved

Published by Boyds Mills Press, Inc.
A Highlights Company
815 Church Street
Honesdale, Pennsylvania 18431
Printed in China

Publisher Cataloging-in-Publication Data (U.S.)

Longfellow, Henry Wadsworth, 1807–1882.
    Paul Revere's ride / by Henry Wadsworth Longfellow ; illustrated by
Monica Vachula ; historical note by Jayne Triber.—1st ed.
[32] p. ; col. ill. ; cm.
Notes: An illustrated version of Longfellow's classic poem about Paul Revere.
ISBN 1-56397-799-0
1. Revere, Paul, 1735–1818—Juvenile poetry. 2. Lexington, Battle of, 1775—
Juvenile poetry. 3. Children's poetry, American. (1. Revere, Paul, 1735–1818—
Poetry.
2. Lexington, Battle of, 1775—Poetry. 3. American poetry. 4. Narrative poetry.)
I. Vachula, Monica. II. Triber, Jayne.
2002105796

First edition, 2003
The text of this book is set in 15-point Stone Serif.

10 9 8 7 6 5 4 3 2 1

Henry Wadsworth Longfellow

(1807–1882)

*L*isten, my children, and you shall hear

Of the midnight ride of Paul Revere,

On the eighteenth of April, in Seventy-five;

Hardly a man is now alive

Who remembers that famous day and year.

He said to his friend, "If the British march
By land or sea from the town tonight,
Hang a lantern aloft in the belfry arch
Of the North Church tower as a signal light—
One, if by land, and two, if by sea;
And I on the opposite shore will be,
Ready to ride and spread the alarm
Through every Middlesex village and farm,
For the country folk to be up and to arm."

*T*hen he said, "Good night!" and with muffled oar
Silently rowed to the Charlestown shore,
Just as the moon rose over the bay,
Where swinging wide at her moorings lay
The Somerset, British man-of-war;
A phantom ship, with each mast and spar
Across the moon like a prison bar,
And a huge black hulk, that was magnified
By its own reflection in the tide.

*M*eanwhile, his friend, through alley and street,
Wanders and watches with eager ears,
Till in the silence around him he hears
The muster of men at the barrack door,
The sound of arms, and the tramp of feet,
And the measured tread of the grenadiers,
Marching down to their boats on the shore.

Then he climbed the tower of the Old North Church,
By the wooden stairs, with stealthy tread,
To the belfry-chamber overhead,
And startled the pigeons from their perch
On the somber rafters, that round him made
Masses and moving shapes of shade—
By the trembling ladder, steep and tall,
To the highest window in the wall,
Where he paused to listen and look down
A moment on the roofs of the town,
And the moonlight flowing over all.

*B*eneath, in the churchyard, lay the dead,
In their night-encampment on the hill,
Wrapped in silence so deep and still
That he could hear, like a sentinel's tread,
The watchful night-wind, as it went
Creeping along from tent to tent,
And seeming to whisper, "All is well!"
A moment only he feels the spell
Of the place and the hour, and the secret dread
Of the lonely belfry and the dead;
For suddenly all his thoughts are bent
On a shadowy something far away,
Where the river widens to meet the bay—
A line of black that bends and floats
On the rising tide, like a bridge of boats.

Meanwhile, impatient to mount and ride,
Booted and spurred, with a heavy stride
On the opposite shore walked Paul Revere.
Now he patted his horse's side,
Now gazed at the landscape far and near,
Then, impetuous, stamped the earth,
And turned and tightened his saddle-girth;
But mostly he watched with eager search
The belfry-tower of the old North Church,
As it rose above the graves on the hill,
Lonely and spectral and somber and still.
And lo! as he looks, on the belfry's height
A glimmer, and then a gleam of light!
He springs to the saddle, the bridle he turns,
But lingers and gazes, till full on his sight
A second lamp in the belfry burns!

A hurry of hoofs in a village street,
A shape in the moonlight, a bulk in the dark,
And beneath, from the pebbles, in passing, a spark
Struck out by a steed flying fearless and fleet:
That was all! And yet, through the gloom and the light,
The fate of a nation was riding that night;
And the spark struck out by that steed, in his flight,
Kindled the land into flame with its heat.

He has left the village and mounted the steep,
And beneath him, tranquil and broad and deep,
Is the Mystic, meeting the ocean tides;
And under the alders, that skirt its edge
Now soft on the sand, now loud on the ledge,
Is heard the tramp of his steed as he rides.

*I*t was twelve by the village clock,
When he crossed the bridge into Medford town.
He heard the crowing of the cock,
And the barking of the farmer's dog,
And felt the damp of the river fog,
That rises after the sun goes down.

*I*t was one by the village clock,
When he galloped into Lexington.
He saw the gilded weathercock
Swim in the moonlight as he passed,
And the meeting-house windows, blank and bare,
Gaze at him with a spectral glare,
As if they already stood aghast
At the bloody work they would look upon.

You know the rest. In the books you have read,
How the British Regulars fired and fled—
How the farmers gave them ball for ball,
From behind each fence and farmyard wall,
Chasing the red-coats down the lane,
Then crossing the fields to emerge again
Under the trees at the turn of the road,
And only pausing to fire and load.

So through the night rode Paul Revere;
And so through the night went his cry of alarm
To every Middlesex village and farm—
A cry of defiance and not of fear,
A voice in the darkness, a knock at the door,
And a word that shall echo forevermore!
For, borne on the night-wind of the Past,
Through all our history, to the last,
In the hour of darkness and peril and need,
The people will waken and listen to hear
The hurrying hoof-beats of that steed,
And the midnight message of Paul Revere.

Longfellow and Paul Revere's Ride

By Jayne E. Triber, Ph.D.

Henry Wadsworth Longfellow (1807–1882) published "Paul Revere's Ride" in the January 1861 issue of Atlantic Monthly magazine and two years later in *Tales of a Wayside Inn*. He was probably America's most popular poet, read by both children and adults, including President Abraham Lincoln. Longfellow's poem made the patriot-silversmith Paul Revere one of the most famous and inspirational figures in American history.

Writing on the eve of the Civil War, with the country divided by slavery, Longfellow believed that Americans had forgotten that their country was founded on the Revolutionary ideas of liberty and equality. A visit to Boston's Old North Church on April 5, 1860, during which he climbed the tower where the lantern signals were hung on April 18, 1775, moved Longfellow to write "Paul Revere's Ride". He hoped that the example of Paul Revere, an ordinary man who fought for liberty and equality, would remind Americans in the 1860s that they, too, could change history by fighting for those same ideas.

Longfellow was a member of the Massachusetts Historical Society, the grandson of a Revolutionary War general, and the proud owner of a home in Cambridge, Massachusetts, that was once General George Washington's headquarters. But his love of history did not prevent him from changing history for dramatic reasons. Paul Revere's ride was not the impulsive act of one man. It was carefully planned and carried out by Revere, an experienced messenger and spy, along with several other people. Based on spying by Revere and other artisans, patriot leader Dr. Joseph Warren first sent Revere to Lexington on April 16, to warn Samuel Adams and John Hancock of a suspected British plan to either arrest them or to seize military supplies in Concord. When the British left Boston on April 18, Dr. Warren sent Revere across the Charles River to Lexington and another messenger, William Dawes, by a longer land route. Revere had also arranged lantern signals from the Old North Church steeple (one, if the British left by land, and two, if they crossed the Charles River) so that patriots across the river in Charlestown could send a rider to Lexington in case British soldiers arrested Revere or Dawes.

Despite the historical errors, Longfellow was accurate in his description of Paul Revere as a brave patriot who fought for liberty and inspired others by his example.